EARLY BIRD STORIES™

Rolling Pumpkins

Early ★ Reader

First American edition published in 2025 by Lerner Publishing Group, Inc.

An original concept by Heather Pindar

Illustrated by Amy Lane

First published by Maverick Arts Publishing Limited

Licensed Edition
Rolling Pumpkins

Lerner Publications Company
An imprint of Lerner Publishing Group, Inc.
241 First Avenue North
Minneapolis, MN 55401 USA

For reading levels and more information, look up this title at www.lernerbooks.com.

Main body text set in Mikado. Typeface provided by HVD Fonts.

Library of Congress Cataloging-in-Publication Data

Names: Pindar, Heather, author. | Lane, Amy (Amy Rose), illustrator.
Title: Rolling pumpkins / Heather Pindar ; illustrated by Amy Lane.
Description: First American edition. | Minneapolis : Lerner Publications, 2025. | Series: Early bird readers – green (early bird stories) | Audience: Ages 5–9. | Audience: Grades K–1. | Summary: "The fairies and goblins love pumpkins. When the goblins don't plant their own patch, they decide to steal from the fairies. This story helps teach how to make the most of a bad situation"— Provided by publisher.
Identifiers: LCCN 2024009074 (print) | LCCN 2024009075 (ebook) | ISBN 9798765647189 (library binding) | ISBN 9798765661567 (paperback) | ISBN 9798765654071 (epub)
Subjects: LCSH: Readers (Primary) | Pumpkins—Juvenile literature. | Reading—Phonetic method—Juvenile literature. | LCGFT: Readers (Publications).
Classification: LCC PE1119.2 .P568 2025 (print) | LCC PE1119.2 (ebook) | DDC 428.6/2—dc23/eng/20240408

LC record available at https://lccn.loc.gov/2024009074
LC ebook record available at https://lccn.loc.gov/2024009075

Manufactured in the United States of America
1-1010883-53148-4/30/2024

EARLY BIRD STORIES™

Rolling Pumpkins

Heather Pindar

Illustrated by
Amy Lane

Lerner Publications ◆ Minneapolis

Fairies like pumpkins. They make them into lanterns. The pumpkins light up the dark winter nights.

Goblins like pumpkins too.

In the spring, the fairies in the Deep Wood planted their pumpkin seeds.

The goblins on the High Hill did not.

It was too much work.

All summer, the fairies looked after their little pumpkin plants.

The goblins did not.

In the autumn, the fairies' gardens were full.

They were full of lovely, big, fat pumpkins.

In the autumn, the goblins' gardens were full of weeds and garbage.

They felt annoyed. They waited until it was dark and the fairies were asleep.

The goblins crept down the hill.

They put all the fairies'

pumpkins in their cart.

The cart was full.

It was hard to pull it up the hill.

The goblins put the pumpkins in their shed.

It was hard to squash them
all in and shut the door.

The shed door swung open.

One pumpkin rolled out.

Then lots of pumpkins rolled out.

BUMP! BUMP! BUMP!

The pumpkins rolled down the hill.

BUMP! BUMP! CRASH!

The pumpkins smashed into lots of little pieces.

The fairies ran out of their houses.

They saw the trail of smashed pumpkins.

It went from the goblins' shed
to the bottom of the High Hill.

"We can't make lanterns with smashed pumpkins," said a fairy, "but we CAN make soup!"

The yummy smell of the pumpkin soup made the goblins feel annoyed.

But the fairies did not offer the goblins soup.
They gave them seeds.

"We're sorry," said the goblins. "Next spring, we will grow our own pumpkins."

And they did! The next year, there were more pumpkins than ever . . .

. . . and plenty of lanterns and soup

for EVERYONE!

Quiz

1. What do the fairies make pumpkins into?

   a) Bowls

   b) Balls

   c) Lanterns

2. Why did the goblins not plant pumpkin seeds?

   a) They forgot.

   b) It was too much work.

   c) They lost the seeds.

3. Where did the goblins put the fairies' pumpkins?

   a) In their shed

   b) In their houses

   c) In their gardens

4. What did the fairies make with the smashed pumpkins?

a) Pumpkin pie

b) Pumpkin soup

c) Pumpkin salad

5. What did the fairies give the goblins in the end?

a) Salad

b) Pie

c) Seeds

Quiz Answers: 1c, 2b, 3a, 4b, 5c

EARLY BIRD STORIES

Leveled for Guided Reading

COLOR	GRL
Silver	L-P
Gold	K-L
Purple	J-K
Orange	H-J
Green	G-I
Blue	E-G
Yellow	C-E
Red	C-D
Pink	A-C

Early Bird Stories have been edited and leveled by leading educational consultants to correspond with guided reading levels. The levels are assigned by taking into account the content, language style, layout, and phonics used in each book. Visit www.lernerbooks.com for more Early Bird Readers titles!